The Yellow Umbrella

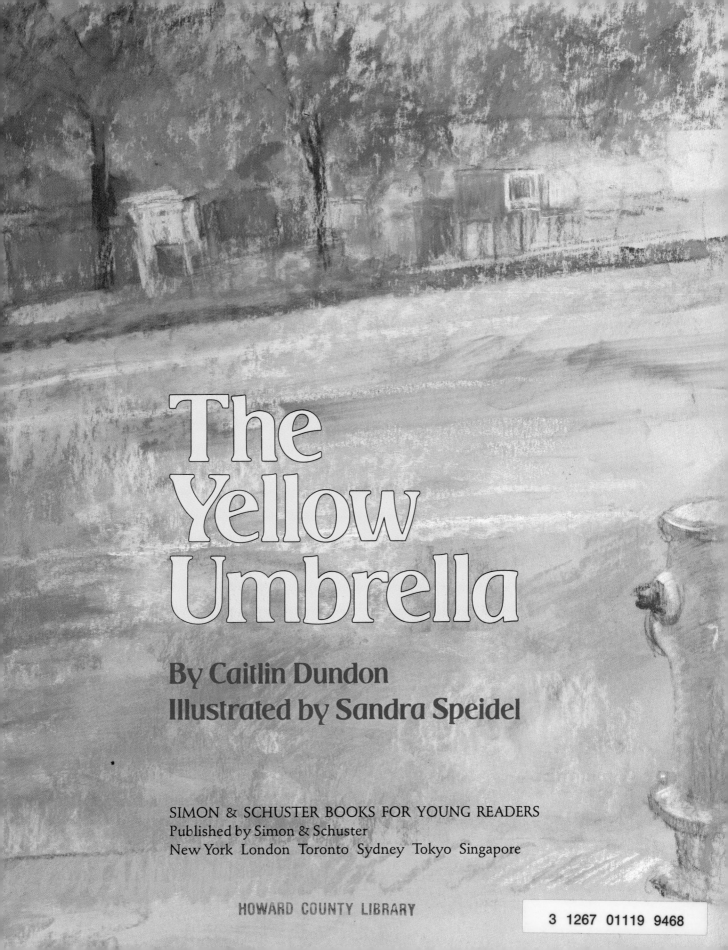

The Yellow Umbrella

By Caitlin Dundon
Illustrated by Sandra Speidel

SIMON & SCHUSTER BOOKS FOR YOUNG READERS
Published by Simon & Schuster
New York London Toronto Sydney Tokyo Singapore

SIMON & SCHUSTER BOOKS FOR YOUNG READERS
Simon & Schuster Building, Rockefeller Center
1230 Avenue of the Americas, New York, New York 10020
Text copyright © 1994 by Caitlin Dundon
Illustrations copyright © 1994 by Sandra Speidel
SIMON & SCHUSTER BOOKS FOR YOUNG READERS
is a trademark of Simon & Schuster.
Designed by Vicki Kalajian.
The text of this book is set in 16 pt. Schneidler Medium.
The illustrations were done in pastel.
Manufactured in the United States of America

10 9 8 7 6 5 4 3 2 1

Library of Congress Cataloging-in-Publication Data
Dundon, Caitlin. The yellow umbrella / by Caitlin Dundon:
illustrated by Sandra Speidel.   Summary: A little boy converts
his mother to the idea of having a bright yellow umbrella
to enjoy in the rain.
[1. Umbrellas—Fiction.]   I. Speidel, Sandra, ill.   II. Title.
PZ7.D915Ye   1993   [E]—dc20   91-44147   CIP
ISBN 0-671-77743-2

To Laurent Linn, who always knew
                              —CD

To my daughter Zoe,
who makes every rainy day
a yellow umbrella day
                              —SS

Once on a very blustery day,
when the rain rained hard
and the wind blew strong,
there was one yellow umbrella
in a sea of hundreds
of boring black umbrellas
bent against the heavy rain
and the strong wind.

People in black raincoats
and gray raincoats and tan raincoats
hurried and hurried against the rain,
hurrying and hurrying
to work in the rain.

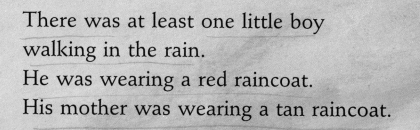

There was at least one little boy
walking in the rain.
He was wearing a red raincoat.
His mother was wearing a tan raincoat.

She was dropping him off at school.
She hurried and hurried against the rain,
hurrying and hurrying to school in the rain.
They were almost late.

She was pulling and pulling on his hand,
trying to hurry his little feet even more.
They were almost late
for school and for work.

But the little boy
had seen something.

There, lying in a gutter
as the rainwater swirled
over and around it,
something yellow.

It was the yellow umbrella,
lying broken in the gutter.

The little boy looked up at his mother,
squeezing her hand as they hurried
and hurried in the rain,
hurrying and hurrying to school
and to work.

"Look, Mama," he said,
"there's a yellow umbrellow."
He pointed with his lunch box
back to the gutter.

"No," said his mother, hurrying,
looking back for only a second.
"It's just a yellow umbrella,"
she corrected him, speaking slowly.

"And stop walking through the puddles,"
she said, not even looking at him.

And they hurried and hurried
through the sideways rain.
They were almost late
for school and for work.

Just as they came around a corner,
so did a big gust of wind.
And the mother's umbrella
was blown inside out and it broke.

"Yella umbrella?" said the little boy.

"Yel-low umbrella," said his mother.
"And stop splashing." And she kept on hurrying,
trying to hold the broken umbrella
in a way that would keep them dry.

At school
there were many umbrellas
of all colors.
Blue ones
and red ones
and orange ones,
and ones with polka dots
and ones with stripes
and ones with flowers
and ones with shapes of all kinds
and even ones with Mickey Mouses.
There were also some black umbrellas
and gray umbrellas
and tan umbrellas,
but they always belonged to the parents
dropping off their children at school.

They were almost late for school
and late for work.
The little boy was still thinking
of something,
something yellow.

"Look, Mama," he said,
pointing with his lunch box.
"There are blue ones
and red ones
and orange ones,
and ones with polka dots
and ones with stripes
and ones with flowers
and ones with shapes
and even ones with Mickey Mouses.
But there aren't any yellow umbrellows."

"Yellow umbrel-las," his mother almost yelled
because of the strong wind. And she watched him as
he went into school, and suddenly she noticed
all the colorful umbrellas—
all the blue ones
and red ones
and orange ones,
and ones with polka dots
and ones with stripes
and ones with flowers
and ones with shapes
and even ones with Mickey Mouses.

Then she noticed
all the smiling children
and all the splashing through puddles
and all the unsmiling parents
and all the black umbrellas
and all the gray and black and tan raincoats,
and all of them hurrying
and hurrying off to work.

She slowly threw her broken umbrella
into a trash can and put up her hood.
Then she walked slowly but steadily
to work. She was already late.

After work it was still raining when she
went to the school to pick up her little boy.

She saw him hurrying out of the doors
exactly on time. And she saw that
he was hurrying because he wanted to,
not because he was late.

Then he saw what she was carrying and he smiled. His mother smiled too, and she kissed his wet cheek and they started walking home together.

But it was different from the walk to school.
They walked slower and she let him splash through
the puddles as long as other people weren't close by,
and they enjoyed the rain when it rained hard
and they enjoyed the wind when it blew hard—

and most of all they enjoyed
their new yellow umbrella.